Climacterics

Flairs and Glairs

Publication House

"Climacterics"

ISBN No: " 9789391302665"
1st Edition
Language – English and Hindi

Flairs and Glairs
Publication House
Regd. Under MSME Act.

Disclaimer

This is a work of fiction and solely represent the thoughts of the corresponding authors of the articles. Our editors have tried their best to edit the content of all the authors and check the plagiarism.

All the write-ups in this book are unique and are only published in this book.

In case any plagiarism or error is found, only the author is responsible alone, and not the publisher or the Compilers.

Cover Designing and Book Formatting
Shubham Shah and Ishani Agarwal

Acknowledgement

The completion of this undertaking could not have been possible without the participation and assistance of so many people whose names may not all be enumerated. Gratitude towards all the co -authors, those have worked very   hard to make this book to be successful one.

We are very thankful to Flairs And Glairs publication, without whom, this project would never have been possible and who gave us a chance to do this womderful project on CLIMACTERICS , which also helped us in doing a lot of research and we came to know about many new things. Moreover heartfelt thanks to our parents, family, relatives and friends for their continuous support and encouragement towards us in completing this book within the limited time frame. Above all to the Great, Almighty, the author of knowledge and wisdom, for his countless love.

Co Author

Shubham Shah (Founder Flairs and Glairs)
Ishani Agarwal (Co -Founder Flairs and Glairs)
Jyoti Matania (Compiler)
Jayanti Kumari Jha (Compiler)

1. Sushmita Ray Choudhury
2. Priya Singh
3. Ankit Kumar
4. Nimisha Koche
5. Bhumi Mahesh Gupta
6. Arsha S Pillai
7. Tasneem Sheikh
8. Aastha Sonavane
9. Aditi Raj Singh
10. Avneet Kaur
11. Bhagyashree Das
12. Kalamkaar
13. Agrima Viraj
14. Payal Indani
15. Athira.Ck
16. Poojalakshmi.V
17. Ashis Pahi
18. Muskan Sachdeva
19. Minati Bhoi
20. Anjaly Vasudevan Nair
21. Harshitha Nadikuda
22. Rohan Makloha
23. Madhu Singh
24. Aman Kumar
25. Samriddhi Gupta

26. Sattarupa Pandit
27. Barkha Matania
28. Prateek Paul
29. Neha Gupta
30. Vishnupriya P
31. Bhavathareni.T
32. Krish Balani
33. Shambhavi D ubey
34. Kavipriya T
35. Monika.M
36. Dikila Ladingpa
37. Vaishnawi Kumari
38. Akriti Sharma
39. Keerthana.N
40. Dhivyajothi.M
41. Dr Gajal Tayal
42. Chinmayee Biswal
43. Rozy Paul
44. Tanvi Jamwal
45. Mohit Satwani
46. Talima Das
47. Anushin Ray
48. Shivangi Singh
49. Soja Joseph
50. Rushda
51. Harshita Verma
52. Amruta Thakare
53. Kshama Tripathi
54. Atul Kumar
55. Ms Purnima
56. Ms. Ishrat Jahan Noormohammed Khan
57. Smita Kumari
58. N. Krishnaveni
59. Unnati Sharma
60. Aswin D
61. Sayeda Nuzhat Fatma

62. Mohini Keshri
63. Mona Patel
64. Sambardhana Dikshit
65. Shipra Pandey
66. Nafisa Azmin
67. Ananya P. Mishra
68. Payal Kamdi
69. Abhilash Sharma
70. Mohanapriya.K
71. Induprakash Deo Pandey
72. Sadiya Siddiqui
73. Princy Carol Gonslaves
74. Jasmine Panda
75. Simranjeet Kaur

Shubham Shah

(Founder - Flairs and Glairs)

Shubham Shah, an entrepreneur at "Flairs & Glairs" a brand with dynamics in events organizing and cultural educational pan INDIA, is a 26yrs old guy who   recently has entered the digital platform of imprinting emotions. He has initiated with his own open mic platform to help budding poets and aspiring writers under his brand named as "Teekhe Zasbaaat"

He is a commerce graduate from the Bhagalpur City of Bihar. He states Writing has impersonated him since childhood and he has now been writing for over a decade!

Cooking, on the other hand, is his passion! He also mentions, trying out new things just tickles him!

When asked sir, Why SPICY EMOTIONS?

He smiled and added, "agar jasbaat teekhe na ho toh wo jasbaat kahan" Spices are all that blends! So do his words!

As a chef, he presents to you his dish! Hot and freshly served! Taste it! Feel it! Enjoy it! You can also find his writing in the Book "Teekhe Zasbaaat" and 50+ Co -authored anthologies.

With his passion to explore opportunities across Platforms, he is working with keen devotion and We wish him all the very best for his future ventures.

He is Featured in the International Magazine DeMode for his upcoming solo novel.

He is Approved by Ne8x for its Lit Fest, and is a Golden Star Awards 2020 Winner.

He is a India Book of Records Holder for his Anthology Satrang, and has the Grandmaster title by Asia Book of Records, for the same.

He has also been featured in Prabhat Khabar, Dainik Jagran, and a lot of other Newspapers in Bihar for his achievements.

He has been a proud co-author to

India Book Of Records (Title- Black)

World Book Of Records (Title -15 Wonders of Poetries)

India Book Of Records (Title - Aaina)

Vajra World Records Holder (Title - Gustakhi Maaf Hai)

High Range of Records Holder (Title - Gustakhi Maaf Hai)

Indian Book of Records

(Title - Road from Worst to Best)

Share your reviews on his

INSTAGRAM

@spicy_emotions
@shubham4shah

Or via email on

shubham2shah@gmail.com

To stay tuned to his work and opportunities follow his business
Handles

INSTAGRAM   FACEBOOK   YOUTUBE

@flairsandglairs
@teekhezasbaaat

WEBSITE:

https://flairsandglairs.in/
https://flairsandglairs.com/

Ishani Agarwal

(Co-Founder- Flairs and Glairs)

Ishani Agarwal hails from the City of Joy, Kolkata.
She is the co -founder of her Community "Teekhe Zasbaaat" and Flairs and Glairs Publication.
Been a Compiler for 45+ Anthologies, she is in the process for more. Co-authored in 150+ Anthologies. She is a India Book of Records Holder, a Vajra World Records H   older, a High Range of Records Holder, an OMG Book of Records Holder, a Bravo Record holder, a Forever Star Book of World Records and an Indian Book of Records Holder.
Approved by Ne8x for its Lit Fest 2020, and Literary Icon 2020. Also a Golden Star Awards Winner 2020.
She has also been awarded with India Star Republic Award 2021, a part of She Awards by Awards Arc and Winner of Nari Samman 2021 by Literoma.

She is also selected as Best Achiever of the Year by AwardsArc and Most Challenging Compiler Award by Spectrum Awards.
She got her first solo Published,a solo Compilation consisting of first 750 contents of hers, titled "Hand That Burnt While Healing".

She has been featured by the National Magazine "Taree Zameen Par" with the title 'unstoppable'.
Also featured in the International Magazine DeMode for her upcoming solo novel, she is proud to write on social issues, and is happy with the love she is receiving.
Connect with her on Instagram: @Ishani_agarwal_quotes / @compilations_so_far

Jyoti Matania
Compiler

Born and brought up in Odisha, Jyoti is currently pursuing her bachelors in political science .Being co -authored in 30+anthologies and in the process of being more ,her 1st anthology"Fierce Fearless 'n' Flawed " is live now. The title "Aaj ki Womaniya ", 'The real heroes' ,'Kalinga Kanya'aptly justifies her essence of being the best version of herself..A national debator,fashionista &yes now a writer..has allowed to be ME! Literature honours her with Sahityakosh samman &Tagore commemorat ive honouree which further allows her to keep inspiring the generation with her work. Celebrating yourself the way you   are has allowed her to be voice for the voiceless and carry herself ..Uh can connect her on her insta handle theroyal_mataniagirl

Lets Save That Peace

Continual Climate Changes, Causing continuity in catastrophes...
Some say these are the end times,
that the battle lines that circumscribe
this globe on which on which we all reside
are drawing too close together;

Like isobars they show too much pressure building, until nothing can survive..

You and I we like being at war with each other
The windy profil es on clothes
on the clothesline and how rain might come soon..
Heat sucks;
Because of the weather you say,I've forgotten everything important.
LETS SAVE THAT PEACE!!

Jayanti Kumari Jha
Compiler

Her name is Jayanti Kumari Jha. She is currently   pursuing her bachelor's degree in commerce. Born in Bihar and brought up in Odisha. She loves simplicity as this makes her personality more expressive. She loves Debating, travelling, enjoying music and writing.   She has been Co -authored in more than 1 5 Anthologies and many more to participate and also being the compiler of 4 Anthologies. Her 1st anthology "Smile : A Strongest Sword is live now."

She believes to Dream high, Fly high and Be high with a lively heart. Being real and unique dignifies her charact er.

Make A Change To Sustain The Beauty

Continual climate changes , causing continuity in catastrophes...
Climate change , a necessary and unavoidable change.
We always aspire to change things , despite knowing about its consequences.
No doubt climate change is the need of hour and it would be good for us if it happens without human disturbances or else we have to pay for it.
Busy schedule and comfort life has increased the stress of nature " BECAUSE WE WANT MORE INSTEAD OF GIVING MORE."
Polar ice shields are melting and the sea is rising. Thereby making our life in danger to sustain.
Changes observed in the Earth's climate i   s mostly due to human activities. Burning fossil fuels , greenhouse gas , heat waves and many more bring extreme harm to our home planet.
It's our responsibility to have a control over everything which harms our environment.   In order to save the beauty then we should care about its survival.
So we must "MAKE A CHANGE TO SUSTAIN THE BEAUTY…"

Sushmita Ray Choudhury

Continual Climatic Changes, causing continuity in catastrophes …
Destroying everything till it becomes left nothing
Is what we've always enjoyed the most!
Cutting down trees which provides us oxygen and food
Will be once no longer anymore!
Abusing water bodies where there is available
Some bodies dies in some places due to lack of resources!
Growing 2 trees after cutting millions
Is that LOVE FOR ENVIRONMENT!!!

Priya Singh

Continual climate changes , causing continuity in catastrophe s…
Though everything seems out of control & we can't do anything about it as it's a Natural calamity

Nothing works as a country until & unless every citizen should feel as hungry

Everyone seems supporting as Family together we have to deal with this I ag ree,

Never try playing with Nature, it would always throw people upto gravity.

Since Earth is part of galaxy
how it couldn't be a part of study,

As everything evolves as tragedy
and cause of all I'm losing my vanity.

Ankit Kumar

Continual climate changes , causing continuity in catastrophes …

लगातार हो रहे जलवायु परिवर्तन विनाश का कारण है

"जलवायु परिवर्तन"

जितना लिया प्रकृति से करो उतना वापस ज़रूर
इसी परस्पर सहयोग का था हमें गुरूर

वक़्त बदला बदली जरूरत करने लगे दोहन
जलवायु हाथ जोड़ चिल्ला रहा बचा लो मोहन

कट रहे पेड़ आ रही है भूकंप और बाढ़
सावन गर्म जेठ में बारिश ठंडा हुआ आषाढ़

अब भी समय है सम्भाल लो प्रकाश को
लगाओ पेड़ बचाओ प्रकृति रोक लो विनाश को

Nimisha Koche

Climate Needs To Be Revived

Continual climate changes, Causing continuity in catastrophes …
And we humans here pitifully ,
Loosing all our hopes.

Days going by we are drowning in the water ,
And watching our dear earth to scatter .
God's beautiful creations is loosing hope ,
And what are we doing here after .

We need to be precauti ous ,
Not for others, but for our sake atleast .
Learn to respect our environment ,
And help it rise again f rom east.

Bhumi Mahesh Gupta

' बेईमान मौसम '

Continual climate changes, Causing continuity in catastrophes …

खुद के गुनाह छुपाने थे, लो मिल गया एक मौका जग को!
बिन मौसम बरसात है, इसमें जरूर कोई बात है!

कहा किसीने बेईमान हुआ ये मौसम है, अरे किसीने तो दिया इसे जरूर कोई धोखा है!
मौसम की घुटन को बयां कौन करे, भैंस के आगे अब भागवत कौन करे!

क्या धोखा क्या साजिश है, कैसे इनको बताओ मैं!
खुद करे प्रदुषण जग को, बनाये अतरंगी फिर कहानी ये!

मतलबी ये मुखौटा इंसानी, किसी के ना हो पाएंगे!
इलज़ाम लगा कर दुसरो पर ये, गुनाह खुद के छिपाएँगे!

Arsha S Pillai

The Cry

Continual Climate Changes , Causing continuity in Catastrophes ...
Crying in the cry of Waves Hitting shores, taking life and living.
India cries, in the midst of pandemic
Corona kicks the belly , lungs and mask.
Drought, floods and quakes
India bleeds, but it's fighting back.
Health workers, social workers, Force wi th all their force,
Seamen in Kerala with all their skill, Indians searching life below a mountain
Life above the waves
Life inside every wild fire,
We are struggling but trying to love more
Planting a rose more.
And saying - We love you nature, and one day
You will love Indians back.

Tasneem Sheikh

Efforts Now

Continual climate changes, causing continuity in catastrophes …
Can't we reduce to plant derived plastics beyond planting trees?
Now, time to power your home with renewable energy.
Reduce water waste; walk, cycle, run and skate
Relish the health alongside a safe state.

Aditi Raj Singh

India's Tough Fight...Growth Vs Climate

Continual climate changes , causing continuity in catastrophes … in the world,still we are not concerned about the climate changes.Let's leave about world, talk about India only, according to the reports India will experience decrease in seasonal mean rainfall and an increase in mean and extreme precipitation .This continual climate changes has already shown India it's disastrous form nume   rous times. One of the catastrophes is of Kedarnath dham of Uttarakhand. Yes Kedarnath know as 'lord of field', the land of mahadev had witnessed that 'prachand roop' of Nature in 2013.

"IF WE ARE STILL LEAST INTERESTED IN CLIMATE CHANGE, KEEP POLLUTING A ND DISBALANCING THE NATURE AND WAIT FOR KARMA." As said 'every drop counts', your each and every step will mark a difference. Let us see what we can do regarding this, Starting from home u se refrigerators efficiently , it will not only be helping your ele ctricity bills but also help the environment. conserve water . So here , I would like to conclude this on the note that, 'only when the last tree is cut, only when the last river is polluted, only when the last fish is caught, will they realise that you can't eat money'. "SO STOP THINKING, AND START WORKING".

Aastha Sonavane

Continual climate changes, causing continuity in catastrophes …
Sitting in my balcony I could hear distant ambulance siren,
I could hear sweeping of helpless mother who was holding back tears so her child couldn't see,
I could feel a naive sister sobbing who was overwhelmed by horror and situation,
I could sense a father in tremor and shock thinking about fate of his child. Thinking of on all this all I could wonder About health care professionals.
about their endless dedication,
About their unswerving spirits,
About their families, about their loved ones,
Risking own life to save others.
So I hope this dark, tragic, catastrophic, endless night to ends soon with Sun of happiness and radiance.

Avneet Kaur

Continual Climate changes, causing continuity in catastrophes… which may seem beautiful or say give a sense of achievement to humans after they exploit nature for their own means, is a mirage for destruction. Climate change is a very dangerous threat to al l the species living on earth, it affect not only animals, plants, but also humans but humans aren't ready to accept that. Humans are so blinded by 'development' that they choose to completely neglect the harm they are causing to nature, which results in c limate changes and disasters. Many factors are responsible for climate changes, some of which include increase in human population, increase in number of factories, deforestation, killing animals etc.

One of most recent and threatening disaster is, indeed , the Corona virus, also known as, the Covid -19. Deforestation have now become a major aspect for lack of fresh air and causing lungs problems to most humans. Plants, animals and all the species have an equal right on earth, as of humans, but humans have b ecome brain dead, neglecting all these factors and now facing all the consequences. It's high time that we start honoring our nature and control climate change, adopting the methods and techniques to sustainable development, or this kind of development mig ht be the possible reason of the fall of human civilization.

Bhagyashree Das

" Atlas Of Our Changing Environment"

Continual climate changes , causing continuity in catastrophes…Throughout Earth's history,climate has continually changed . Even if climate change can also have natural causes,it is largely related to human activity and greenhouse gases.The cause of current climate change is largely human activities , like burning fossil fuels, natural gas,oil and coa l.Burning these materials releases what are called greenhouse gases into Earth's atmosphere . The cause is the increase in greenhouse gases of human origin,with the consequences of health,ecological and humanitarian crises of which we are seeing the beginn ings.

Global temperatures and sea levels are rising,and possibly contributing to larger more devastating storms.The data shows the earth is warming and it's up to us to make the changes necessary for a healthier planet. Some preventive measures that we ca n take to reduce climate changes are - Renewable energies,Waste management and recycling,Sea and ocean preservation,Circular economy,Sustainable transportation and most importantly to get rid of pollution. Climate changes affects everyone ! It's our job a s a community to help prevent climate change!

Kalamkaar

जलवायु परिवर्तन

Continual Climate Changes causing continuity in catastrophes...

बदलते जलवायु परिवर्तन से हो रहा लगातार विनाश
भूकंप के कहर से लोगो का बचना दुस्वार हो गया है!
जलवायु के परिवर्तन होने से केहरे ये हो रहा है!
मकान टूट रहे सब बेघर होते जा रहें है!
हो रही वर्षा तो वही घर डूबे जा रहें है!
मौत का तांडव ना जाने क्यों ऐसा हो रहा है!
इस मुश्किल वक़्त में भी कहर जलवायु परिवर्तन का विकराल रूप ले रहा है!
लोगो का जीवन संकट में आप रहा है!
मौत के कुएँ में जैसे जीवन बीत रहा है!

Agrima Viraj

Steps For Sustainability

Continual climate changes, causing continuity in Catastrophes… Hindering humanity due to the lagging literacies
Increasing insecurities instead of equitable equalities
Let us try to control consumptions and provoke productions
Ensuring end to poverty an d offering opportunities
to include improved nutrition to the whole nation
Abiding agriculture with growth in economy
Conserving the biodiversity to withstand water bodies
Take a stepping stone in making our country contemporary

Payal Indani

Reality Check..

Continual climate changes, causing continuity in catastrophes… is a huge and massive problem in today's world. From humans to animals, weather changes have hit us hard. Even the pandemic could be one of the reason of such catastrophe. People take it casual ly when it comes to protect the environment. All the concern arises, when they themselves are in the trap of such catastrophe. Unwanted disasters destroy the whole beauty of nature and leave us with the barren land. Sooner, we will be facing all such disasters in our daily routine. We really need to look after our unprotected actions so that we can save our mother earth and live peacefully.

Athira.C K

Gleam Of Prospect

Continual climate changes, causing continuity in catastrophes…
Breeze is whispering the echoes of jeopardy
Gloom wrappes the cheek of twilight
when the consequences of human activities cover to them
then nature copies the colour of rainbow
the boundaries of nature leads the mankind to move on
they are walking thro ugh summer of life realities
they swim in the torrent of crisis
after the conflict of autumn the new rays of prospect will touch the seed
the journey of the roots ends in the smell of soil
when treat the nature softly it will give birth to spring..

Poojalakshmi. V

The Fate Which Burdens

Continual climate changes , causing Continuity in catastrophes…
Hardens everyone's day to day life
A great impact which
Burdens us in distinct ways
Don't know the way to survive
But till not lost our path
Till not tired to protect our motherland...

Ashis Pahi

Struggle:

Continual Climate Changes, causing continuity in catastrophes… It's true no doubt. What is going on in this world nobody knows and what has to occur nobody knows as well. The way we are preferring to survive in this world similarly the upcoming generation must be feeling the same the way we are thinking. But, the way the climatic conditions of the glaciers, human stamina, and strength with capabilities are decreasing, unexpected pandemics hit the whole world, up -gradation of 5G network making problem to the birds and for the tree, cities are getting into the worst scenario. What can be done? Any idea, obviously everyone has an idea but doesn't have the power to rectify it.

If we will plant trees in place of those areas where trees were cut down by Govt for the widening of the road. By cutting down trees many people are facing sun   -stroke and climatic impact gradually increasing and its impact can be seen in Glaciers and the Tropical regions. People are preferring to work more in the corporate sector and   they can't focus on their health so that they are also facing lots of diseases. Upgradation is necessary similarly we have to look forward to those birds who stay in the air due to microwave they are facing problem while flying above and its impact can be seen in trees.

Muskan Sachdeva

Kedarnath

Continual Climate Changes , causing continuity in catastrophes…
Clouds bursting, rain falling
All thought is a normal rain as always
But no one knew everything will be changed after this day
Everything turned into black
Everything shattered within some time
That's how climate lead to catastrophe......

Minati Bhoi

Climate Change Is Making India Less Livable.

Continual climate changes, causing continuity in catastrophes … We are facing so many kinds of problems due to climate change. We are also not feeling well. For this disasters happen. In other words we are also responsible for this. Man -made disasters, pollutions wh ich destroy our planet. Our earth is facing so many problems.
We make air,water,soil pollutions. We are doing what should we love, but we don't think what should it does in our future. These disasters destroy our plants and animals. Animals have lost thei r shelters. Pollutions make skin problems and it will affect our respiratory system. And it also causes global warming. High temperature on earth surface. Green house effect this is a process which warms our earth's surface. Climate change mainly affect ou r farmers life. Because they are depend on climate for their crops. They are also facing troubles. They want a plenty of rain fall for their crops, but it's not possible because of this. Nothing comes according to their planning. So we should take steps to control this. Keep our environment clean and healthy, don't use costly things and don't waste food. And don't make so many pollutions. Live happily .

Anjaly Vasudevan Nair

Lost River And Lost Happiness

Continual climate changes , causing continuity in catastrophes … Maria thought as she walked through the dry river. Its the same river once gave her blissful happiness. She used to play there in her childhood but now drought taken away the river and her happiness too. Being a nature lover Maria always tried to enjoy the beauty that surrounds her but now there is no beauty only dried lands, struggling farmers and the women who walk kilometers to collect water are the pictures around her. She slowly moved towards a small rock and sat on that, there was a tree nearby but it has no leaves only dried branches. She pull out the water bottle from her back pack. Pouring some water into soil for the tree and drinking the remaining she started to read an article which described the cause and eff ect of climatic changes. As she finished reading she looked at the dead tree and parched river once again. Then she hold the article tight to her chest. Tears were forming in her eyes and questions were raising in her head. All she could see was a hopeless   generation at the verge of winning and losing life.
"Its already late now. Mom would get panic. Maybe she would have gone for collecting water too"
She thought as she kept walking again.

Harshitha Nadikuda

Continual Climatic Changes, causing continuity in catastrophes…
This calamity have the chronical consequences of catharsis too.

The catastrophes are the circumlocution that Earth is being exploited completely,
So, it's complusary to cease the contamina tion caused to the nature,
By conserving the natural resources.

Now it's must to be a cognizant and circumspect regarding,
Be concerned about our Climatic Changes,
And certainly we can come across the peaceful climate of our past.

Rohan

Wreak Havoc

Continual climate changes, causing continuity in catastrophes...
Humans, losing the earth,
With all it's abilities.
Audacity enough is there to colonize Mars,
Leaving behind the Mother Earth,
In the situation harsh. What If,
the change fastens?
What if, early actions become too late?
Let us start Now,
Let us start together,
Forgetting the every Hate.
Promises official are reminiscent enough,
That the planet belongs to every Life born over it.
But due to our arbitrary de eds to get developed,
A wreak havoc named Climate Change hover it.

Madhu Singh

"Continual Climate Changes , Causing Continuity In Catastrophes…"
Human Activities Are The Biggest Cause Of Climate Changing,Coz They Burn Plastics Fossil Fuels And Cut Trees And This Is The Thing Which Makes Crisis On Our Earth And Cause Of This Our Earth Suffering From Covid.
Sometimes Our Decisions Makes Our Earth Worst, We Reduced Agricultural And Get Health Issues In Cities Du   e To Heat And Some Other Things....
The Things Which Happens Due To Climate Changing Are The,...... (Health Issues, Farming, Pure Air, Deforestation And Permafrost And Etc.)

AMAN KUMAR

Continual climate changes , causing continuity in catastrophes…
"चाहत किसी चाहत का कम नहीं होता,
जो बांध लेते चाहत को जीवन सुखमयी होता"।

पहले कदमों से रास्तों को नापा करते, दिल- दिमाग, शरीर सब से शक्तिपूर्ण रहते,
जैसे ही राहत के लिए पशु गाड़ी लाये, फिर वो राहत लोभ इंधन में बदल गये। होते थे जो काम हाथों से,
अब मशीनों से काम लेते, जंगलों को साफ कर बसाया शहर,
फिर भी सुकून ना मिला तो दौड़ा दिया मोटरवाहन सड़क पर। बदल रही है प्रकृति का रंग रूप,
बेवक्त होने लगी हैं शर्दी, गर्मी और बरसात, अनाजों के उपज में भी मिलाने लगे रसायन,
हवा को दुषित कर अब भूमि को प्रदुषित करने लगे।
"बढ़त बढ़त लोभ बढ़त, नाश समीप होय।
अब भी जो ना पहचाने, फिर कुछ हाथ में ना होय"।।

Samriddhi Gupta

We The Liable Beings

Continual climate changes , causing continuity in catastrophes…
We are the only ones who are
responsible for these undesirable causes

Save water, Plant more trees
Take care of the surroundings
Should be the main goal
For us to preserve the nation being human beings.

Sattarupa Pandit

Continual climate changes, Causing continuity in catastrophe s....
In this modern era of 21st century, lives and lifestyles of people are swirling in a higher rate. In such an developing time, the destruction level is on the top . And this   give a special attention towards our environment. Deforestation and global warming are the most highlighted topics now.
The continuous cutting down of trees, rapid growth in the industrial sector, rapacious use of natural resources are rapidly dragging ou r mother earth to the edge of destruction. No doubt our life is getting easier day by day but in order to get an easy life we are discomforting the animals, natural resources and cutting down of trees. Ignoring that they are our saviors. The increase in gl obal warming and deforestation are resulting in increase in natural calamities such as Tsunami, cyclone, forest fire, floods, glacier melts, land slidings and a great increase in sea level. It is epitomely said that "happiness lies, first of all in health"   and "health is the true wealth". We should and must protect our environment and do plant more and more trees, awake the people and aware the people about the destructions.
"The earth is the mother of all and all should have equal rights upon it" ...."Live and let live"

Barkha Matania

Continual Climate Changes   , causing Continuity in Catastrophes…

The earth is in a death spiral. We the citizens are running the most dangerous experiment in history right now which is to see how the atmosphere has also   become a crucial part in spreading the CORONA VIRUS pandemic.We need to find out the ways before there is an environmental catastrophe.Recently Greta Climate Change Speech was making headlines.Greta Tunberg,a 16 year old teenager got the chance to speak a t the UNCAS.Remember?We have been made to write essays on Climate change since our school days but...nothing changed.Now,we have the titanic fame,LEONARDO DI CAPRIO,speaking about climate change in his Oscar speech.

Twenty five years ago people could be e xcused for not knowing or doing much about climate change.But today when the Indian scientists have even found out the vaccine of CORONA VIRUS that the world is suffering from more than 1 year we cannot give excuse regarding climate change.I hold a vision of this blue green planet. We are ready to make the next leap -as momentous as giving vote to women. Only spreading awareness isn't the answer.Its time to act,as actions yield results..

Prateek Paul

Climacterics: Take Control… Before It Is Too Late.

Continual Climate Changes, causing continuity in catastrophes… are creating big havoc in the present universe. Many natural calamities have been taking place unexpectedly. Every day we hear news of catastrophes such as cloud burst, landslides, avalanches, famine, earthquakes, volcanos, etc. Have you ever wondered who is to blame for everything? Of course, we the humans. To establish our supremacy over nature, we have forgotten that we are only puppets in the hands of nature. If we play with it, we have to pay for it. The mad rush of modernization has left us with the after -effects of our own mistakes. The more and more luxurious modern lifestyle, the more and more change in a climatic pattern leading to more and more severe consequences. If we want to avoid these catastrophes, we will have to live according to what nature has decided for us, without trying to change it. Only this alone can save humans. Time has come when we sit calmly and think of living a lifestyle as our ancestors used to live. We must reme mber the words of Gandhiji "The world has enough for everyone's needs, but not everyone's greed." Let not our greed destroy us. Let us realize this before it is too late.

Neha Gupta

Covid - 19 - A Killer Of Humanity

Continual Climate Changes, causing continuity in catastrophes…
Continually climate changes,
Causing continuity in catastrophe.
Every citizen faced devastation,
As ambience turned into nasty.

Drought and flood end up with dilapidated,
Corona seize breathe of delighted souls.
Pollution level caused bronchial diseases,
Tainted water adds to diarrhoeal diseases.

Continually climate changes,
Causing continuity in catastrophe.
We can head out of it,
Just by geared up with prophylactic steps.

Vishnupriya P

The Endless Knot

Continual climate changes   , Causing continuity in catastrophes …
All I wanted was escape from this torrdity but this numbness in my veins!
I built domicile for my generation and for the next generation
My preservings ruined the breath and freedom of my generation
The roof I built for them destroyed the roof of the earth
The dilapidated roof eagerly welcomed the sun's heat
They turned the earth into a fireball
That day I looked back for the first time and in despair I realized that I had amassed ruin for them

Bhavathareni. T

Stain Of Darkness

Continual Climate Changes   , Causing Continuity In Catastrophes …
Invented Light To Prevent Darkness
Summer Turnup Heat - Temporary
Signs No Turning Back - Coal
Born To Burn But Now - Earth
Burning Will Keep Burning - Makes
Our Life Stain Of Darkness...

KRISH BALANI

Climate Changes And Development

Continual climate changes, causing continuity in catastrophes… The climate has been continuously changing due to human interference in natural processes. Agreements like Kyoto Protocol(1997) and the Paris Agreement(2015) have been brought into action by UN FCC but these did not show effective results. These protocols sometimes prove as barriers in development of the country. Preventive measures include afforestation, use of renewable energy, investment in energy -efficient technology, limited digging of Earth while mining etc. We should keep our motherland green and clean .

Along with it, we should use least non -renewable resources and more renewable resources. An example of this is use of sunlight instead of coal for producing electricity. Investments should be made in developing new technologies that make effective use of renewable energy and it will be helpful. Digging deep inside the Earth while mining leads to increase in surface temperature , global warming. We should try our best to avoid such climatic ch anges. It will be the best gift that we can provide to our next generations. They should also experience the best part of our nature. So, stop harassing the nature and let the climate change naturally.

Shambhavi Dubey

Growth V/S Climate

Continual Climate Changes , causing continuity in catastrophes… We read every day about the desecration of our environment and the mismanagement of our natural resources. We have always had the capacity to wreck the environment on a small or even regional   scale. Centuries of irrigation without adequate drainage in ancient times converted large areas of the fertile valleys into barren desert. What is new is that we now have the power to change our global environment irreversibly, with profoundly damaging effects on the robustness and integrity of the planet and the heritage that we pass to future generations.

This we know: the earth does not belong to man: man belongs to the earth.... Whatever befalls the earth, befalls the sons of the earth. Man did not wea   ve the web of life: he is merely a strand in it. Whatever he does to the web, he does to himself, therefore for Fairness to Future Generations we, the human species, hold the natural environment of our planet in common with all members of our earth.

Kavipriya T

H2o

Continual climate changes, causing Continuity in catastrophes ...
H2O destroyed dam,
River substracted from its path,
The wind lashed out the trees,
Where to live, where to die,
There is only rainy smokey sky,
Rain go away; come another day...

Monika. M

Continual climate changes , Causing continuity catastrophes…
Years of drought, devour lives
Seized the lush shore
Seed remains seed,
Being arid and withered
Earth shed tears for drizzle...
Myths and spirits for the
Baffling mystery of aridity.

Dikila Ladingpa

Era Of Cessation

Continual Climate Changes, causing continuity in Catastrophes …
Ceaseless liberating harmful gases in the atmosphere Greenhouse effect contributing the climate change with largest share
Deliberately causing depletion of Ozone layer Regardless in the name of growth "Alas, human conceal extremity fear

Let's join hands and work together for better future Shrink carbon pro file, rethink plane,train and automobile to stop planet rapture
Reduce waste and drive brain for fuel efficient vechile help the nature to nurture
The voice of yours, preventive measures, creativity growth along with conservation is to secure and cease f   utile expenditure.

Vaishnawi Kumari

Continual Climate Changes , causing continuity in
catastrophes…
Everyday is a new dawn
The weather changes as well ..
Know how these seasons are changing. And giving us new
diseases...
Where there is a need to plant trees, we are cutting trees and
fulfilling our needs. Where we need pure air, we are
spreading pollution
Where all these things affect us? How the weather changes
in a moment.
And brings with it many diseases not known as change
Today some similar disaster has come to us
Life has stopped due to shortage of breath People are losing
their lives due to shortness of breath...
Neither we make the mistake of cutting down trees, nor   do
we have to see this day
So swear that every day from today onwards Plant a new
plant and make our environment clean

Akriti Sharma

Continual climate change s , causing continuity in catastrophes …

It is due to the increasing global surface temperature a possibility of more Droughts and increased intensity of storms will likely occur. Continual Climate changes due to increase in average global temperature . Today India is facing its toughest fight betw een growth and climate .If we throw light on our Climate condition it is forced due to increasing of colds and the flu and among the most common viral infection is COVID -19 today. The COVID -19 pandemic and associated health and economic crises .

In 2020-2021 India is Facing many Difficulties due to pandemic as well India Is on the top countries who is facing too dangerous problem both in economic growth and Climatic change. This climatic change push to the bad condition in this pandemic to the health of the   people. As India is In developing countries list and the most drawback is that India Has not developed yet is the debate issue on Unemployment in India and the Growth rate is Less in India of Employment and literacy growth. These two Factor i.e, Growth and Climate are Main issue for the discussion and how we can improve it.

keerthana. n

Nature's Deed

Continual Climate Changes , Causing continuity in catastrophes…
Unpredictable at times
And unbearable at times.
Is this nature's deed
In return for man's selfish greed.
What should be done
To turn these catastrophes into none.
To not be a sinner who is unforgiven
Should we protect her Children,
By conserving the forests
And the enchanting coral reefs.
Will these make her calm,
Before we get struck in a strom.

Dhivyajothi.M

Make It Possible

Continual climate change s, causing continuity in catastrophe s…
A major reason for this crisis is we "Humans". We are killing our own planet, we are the major destroyers. We people should be aware and take all possible measurements to save our planet from catastrophe. We are destroying our own bio diversity by creating pollution, deforestation, power station, burning fossils, using plastics etc. Our grandparents didn't even know about the word "climate crisis", we are the very first generation to feel the effect of climate change. Of course we can't change everything ov ernight, we should be patient and have to reverse everything gradually. The best solution is "to go along with nature and to grow nature". Nature plays a major role in stabilising the climate. The best plan is to go with greens, as a first step we should   plant atleast one sapling in everyone's home. "Tiny drops make ocean" like that our tiny step can make a huge change in our climate. The most important thing is to emit less carbon   . Everything is in our hands , "Nothing is impossible" so, we can definitely make it possible.

Dr Gajal Tayal

Climate And Pandemic

Continual climatic changes, causing continuity in catastroph es....

These changing climate make us more stressed and panic in these pandemic situations as already we are suffering from a global pandemic. It's difficult for us to survive during climate change. But how can we forget these changes are just result of human activities means our gree   dy activities. Our nature has enough to make us feed but it doesn't have sources to full fill our greed or anyones greed.

These climatic changes make us more vulnerable to disease as our immunity gets effected by external agents too. we don't got time to a   dapt and the virus Can easily effect us   . That doesn't mean we can't fight and win or we can't take any preventive measures. We should eat healthy food and daily burn our calories through exercise and had a limited food according to our digestion capacity.   we should follow daily proper routine and because of all these, we can make ourselves healthy and happy. So, at last I want to say that "please follow all preventive measures.so,that we can lead our normal life again after recovering from this pandemic and can adapt ourselves in climate changes"

Chinmayee Biswal

"Continual climate changes, causing continuity in catastrophes ..."
Climate change is real, and the evidence is all around us. While the changes to the earth's climate are nothing new, it is apparent recent effects are having a devastating impact on countless people, places, and wildlife. Climate changes usually refers to the shifts in things like precipitation, wind patterns, and temperatures over a given period.
CAUSES OF CLIMATE CHANGE: Cli mate change has now become a greatest threat to our society . Climate change is accelerating are Green house gases,solar activity, agriculture, deforestation, human activity, livestock etc.
IMPACT OF CLIMATE CHANGE: The long term impact of climate change could be absolutely devastating to the planet. While some nations around the world are taking action with initiatives such as the Paris Climate Agreement, others are continuing business as usual –pumping millions of tons of carbon into the atmosphere year after year. While the long-term consequences are still to be seen, for now, climate change continues to cause extreme weather as well as safety and economic challenges on a global scale.

Rozy Paul

"Continual climate changes, causing cont inuity in catastrophes…"
Big challenge - Climate change is big challenge for world.This is not only for India it is a big problem for world also how to mitigate the problem or reduce the risk of problems which causes fire forest,flood,land erosion,cyclone,d rought even many diseases happen due to this climate change.This is not a simple problem this is very serious problem and people should take it seriously and act upon on this.Reduce use of plastics, use recycling or biodegradable single use plastic,use clo thes bag, help other living creatures to live.If many creatures extinct from the world whoever help us to balance this ecosystem.
This universe can't survive only the well being of human we need to balance among others who helped to gather clouds,who helpe d for clean up remains of others garbage.We are in serious problem but we don't understand the situation and don't act on that.But this is high time and we have to cooperate to fight this climacteric changes and it's severe consequences which effects is ve ry hard.

Tanvi Jamwal

Globe, Global Warming And Growth

Continual climate changes, causing continuity in Catastrophes… first of all, we all need to understand that what is climate crisis ? Climate crisis is a term describing global warming and climate change, and their consequences. This Cataclysmic situation has made all of us stand between life and death. India is seventh most affected by climate change in 2019 globally. Report between 2000 and 2019, over 475,000 people lost their li ves. Certain disasters, problems that we are facing such as many types of dis asters, including storms, heat waves, floods and droughts   , insect outbreaks all linked to climate crisis had increased wildfire. If we talk about changes in growth due to climate crisis the natural disasters are happening which is not good so regarding tha t various agreements have been signed . Following are some suggested measures :
• Protecting poor and vulnerable sections through an inclusive and sustainable development strategy   .
•   Achieving national growth through ecological sustainability.
• Devising efficient and cost -effective strategies.

Mohit Satwani

"Continual climate changes, causing continuity in catastrophes…"
India is facing a continual climate changes due to serve polution . this is just because of our bad habits of using resources in a worse way. we use them continously like when we are just going to buy a milk from shopkeeper which is located out of the stre et we take a vechile for it. when we are on signal our vechiles are on . we rushely cutting the tree so what about the nature . nature will respond on that .and results are on board now. but we are still blaming each other for the results and continuously doing the same activity again and again. we have to come together to fight against this problem if no one is changing just change yourself and work it out . the god is given a beautiful gift the nature never destroy this gift because if we doesnot value th e good gift of god he will provide a gift that our current behaviour deserves.

Talima Das

Love Our Nature

Continual climate changes, causing continuity in catastrophes… Human beings are responsible for these changes in the environment. So these should be rectified by humans. For rectification, firstly we should love our nature including all the living beings.   We should plant more and more trees. Trees have the ability to protect us from all the environmental catastrophes. We should conserve the forests, wild life and water. We should educate the unaware people. Everyone should be aware of our environment.

Anushin Ray

Increasing Environmental Issues Owing To Development: The Indian Scenario

Continual climate changes , causing continuity in catastrophes … India is developing in all aspects and spheres. Targeting socio -economic development, rapid industrialization and urbanization has been taking place. Development consequently has led to several environmental issues. Severe air, water and land pollution; stress on natural resources and increased mining; loss of biodiversity; and also enhancing global warming and climate change and much catastrophes.

However, poverty reduction and betterment of society is not possible without economic growth. This is why we need an economic growth with different economic, social and ecological qualities, like high economic dynamism, and ecological sustainability - the Green Growth Approach. The paradigm shift is possible when government, policy makers, industries, corporates, and, in dividual citizens, become more conscious and plunge into action. Industries ought to become more eco -friendly. The public needs to understand that 'concrete over natural landscape' is not at all a sign of healthy development. Preserving Nature is feasible, and reverting Climate Change too, and with our willingness much more can be done.

Shivangi Singh

The Change...

Continual climate changes, causing continuity in catastrophes…"
Slowly the moment passed,
Holy the heart asked, Is it necessary?
Vanishing a whole pure identity,
And turning it into an absolute different entity,
Neither can I nor can the almighty,
Going to be able to stop it, Is it really necessary?

Welcoming a new world of unexpected aff airs,
Running away from the old self,
Is something that means one's changed,
The one who will survive at any range,
Eternal is the change, the change is sustained,
Return what you take, the nature is explained.

Soja Joseph

Fight With Disasters

Continual Climate Changes , Causing Continuity In Catastrophes…
whether rich or poor both are suffering same mental frustration . never lose your sense of power. miserable times will passaway but self recovery is more important .instead of being depressed find the measures to tackle this pandemic outbreak.our nation's growth is in our hands.natural calamities taken away the dreams of many souls so show some gesture to the people who needs your kind .government can take initiatives in cou nseling programmes through medias. it helps to refresh the weak mind of peoples. rules are for our safety it can helps to live more days on this earth.take your own responsibility in your health.

Rushda

Save Me!

Continual climate changes, causing continuity in catastrophes…
Unheard cries of mother nature, giving a halt to beautiful earth.
Polluted seas and damaged forests, crying their hearts out for help.
Te human need to grow and grow, destroying them beyond reparations.

O mankind! Sa ve me for your own benefit. Lest you be destroyed.
O child! Hug me again and love me. Lest I die.
I remain unheard for ages and then extinct.
Consider it my request and help me to save you.

Harshita Verma

Nature

Continual climate changes , causing continuity in catastrophes…
A result of growth activities giving way to disasters
No attention given on the climate and what it wants
Excess air and water pollution the result of growth But   the real suffering is of the trees and fishes
The day to day disasters a result of advancements at sake of nature
These could have been easily rectified if acts were done in a proper way
Heed must be given to what the nature has to say.

Amruta Thakar e

Continual Climate Changes , causing continuity in catastrophes… is "HUMAN".
As compare to other countries, Our India is suffering from hazardous, such a Harmful Disaster which really affects to growth of our country. It's just because of Humans. Humans know the reason of climate change. Most of the people's are doing work which di rectly affect to our environment like cutting tree's.The people are educated, know about affects of cutting tree s but they just want to earn mo ney.
Yes it's true and such a n increasing growth of our country like Technology Advancement, but its due to exce ssive, Creatures has start ed destroying and Of course, We Ourselves also. Increasing radiation power in environment, People's are dying. Not only this, there are many reasons which makes too harmful for our earth as well as our lives.
" Everyone Gives the message, Yes, Everyone does it. But, No one try to change this hazardous climate!! " Our India swims between increased population growth, excessive technology advancement and harmful climate changes. If this goes on like this, then the end is sure.

Kshama Tripathi

Continual climate changes, causing continuity in catastrophes…

उठता धुआँ कुछ कुछ रहा है । थमती साँसों का सिलसिला बढ़ रहा है ।

सहर उठी वसुधा भी अब तपन से। रो रही प्रकृति अपने चमन से। विदोहन की प्रक्रिया अनवरत जारी है।न जाने नवीनीकरण की ये कौन सी बीमारी है।

कट रहे हैं वृक्ष, बन रहे है घर। घुल रहा है फिजाओं में हर पल जहर।

बिगड़ती जा रही है मौसमों की गिनती। बढ़ती जा रही है किसानों की बैचेनी ।

संतुलता पर असंतुलता का बोझ भारी है । लगता है इंसानों के विनाश की ये तैयारी है।

अब रोक लो प्रदूषण की इस कहानी को । बना दो अवनी को फिर हरा- भरा ।

जोड़ कर प्रकृति से नाता, कर लो अब खुद से भी ये वादा । करगे प्राकृतिक संसाधनों का उपयोग । लिखेंगे विकास की एक नई परिभाषा।

Atul Kumar

Climate Change Vs Growth In Name Of Development

Continual climate changes , causing continuity in catastrophes…
In name of development we cut the trees.
It reduce the quantity of oxygen in free.
It also the main reason for devastation during the flood.

In name of growth we made buildings .
But we forget about nature that leads to decrease of air quality .
Testing of nuclear weapon more and more lead to earthquake
.

Ms Purnima

....वातावरण को शुद्ध बनाओ....

Continual Climate Changes , Causing Continuity in Catastrophes...
"पेड़ो की कमी है, हर कोने मे
क्यों न लगाए हम पेड़ अनेक"
"पेड़ो को बचाए कुछ इस तरह,हमे जीने को कुछ पल मिल जाए"
"कटते जा रहे ,पेड़ हजार
"प्रदूषण की हो रही जय जयकार"
पेड़ो की कमी है, हर कोने में ,
क्यों न लगाए हम , पेड़ अनेक"

Ms. Ishrat Jahan Noormohammed Khan

Losing Hopes....

Continual Climate Changes   , causing continuity in
catastrophes …
Losing lot of hopes
Making lot of damaged scopes

Lives are getting disturbed
Everyone is getting blurred
Trying to adjust with climate
And live life with their soulmate.

Smita Kumari

Affects Of Climatic Change In India

Continual climatic changes ,   causing continuity in catastrophes…
India is at the top in the list of nations which are worsely hit by the effects of climate change.
There are variations causes they affect the change of climate like variation in the Earth's orbital characteristics, vo   lcanic eruption,atmospheric carbon dioxide variation, plate techtonics etc.
We know that India has a great contribution in the field of agriculture.But due to climatic change ,India is experiencing a suicide epidemic in rural areas.Three 'big five' suicid e states are maharashtra, Andhra pradesh,karnataka,madhya pradesh,Chattisgarh.
India is the world's fourth largest emitter of greenhouse gases .According to a research organization around half of carbon dioxide emissions since 1750 have come from US and Europe.

N. Krishnaveni

Because Nature Is Precious!

Continual climate changes, causing continuity in catastrophes …
It is devastated to see our Mother's fissures and wrinkles.
The selfish giants made the homeland infertile using toxic drugs,
And makes the Earth boils down like a firing -volcano bugs.
Time flees in waiting for the rain to make the fields deep   -green.
But the existing climatic disasters won't change,
Until or un less there are changes in our thoughts of guidelines.
Drop using plastics and pesticide farming rather turn to organic plant breeding.

Unnati Sharma

प्रकृति में बदलाव

Continual climate changes , causing continuity in catastrophes…

(क्यूँ हो रहा जलवायु में बदलाव) क्यूँ हो रहा है हमारी जलवायु में ये बदलाव,

क्यूँ हो रही इस बदलाव से धरती है विरान,

वजह हम खुद हैं इसकी, जो बे मतलब खर्च कर रहे प्रकृति की खान,

बस देख रहे अपनी ही सुविधा और फैला रहें जहरीली गैसें,

पर उनकों फैलाने में हम मानव ही पूरे हिस्सेदार,

और इस कृतिम चीजों से हो रहा वतावरण का सर्वनाश,

वक्त है अभी भी रोक ले खुद को न करें प्रकृति से छेड़छाड़,

वरना कृतिम आक्सीजन भी न बचा पायेगी प्राण...

Aswin D

It's Time To Act!

Continual Climate Changes, causing continuity in catastrophes …

Floods, cyclones, storms all are slamming humans worldwide, causing huge losses. Earth's surface temperature as well as ocean surface temperature has increased, which can lead to the melting of polar ice caps, hurricanes etc. Let's see what we can do:

Control emission of greenhouse gases and replace fossil fuels with renewable energies. According to the Intergovernmental Panel on Climate Changes, global emission should be zero by 2050.   According to the U.N., 14.5% of all greenhouse gas emissions came from   the livestock industry, where beef production contributes to 41%, while milk production contributes to 14%. Restore nature. Forests, mangroves, wetlands etc., can absorb a large amount of greenhouse gas.

And finally, CONSUME LESS. Natural resources are limited, and they will be depleted if not used wisely. Avoid overfishing, over -harvesting etc. The situation is quite catastrophic, and if this continues, we will meet the apocalypse. So, as responsible citizens, let's join our hands for a green planet.

Sayeda Nuzhat Fatma

Continual climate changes, causing continuity in catastrophes …
Climate is going to change, What is happening in strange.
A very big changes came in weather, People are busy in tree's murder.
So,the world faces global warming, Now,acid rain is showering.
There is strict hot in summer, Bone broken cold in winter.
Let take a pledge to save weather, Plant trees more further.
To save the upcoming generation, Awareness should be mention.
Otherwise, uni verse will lost it sustain, If we will not maintain.
*Use more electric vehicles, Stop poisonous air which is rising.
Let us save our environment, Make it beautiful with green tent.

Mohini Keshri

Growth Vs Climate

Continual climate Changes, causing continuity in catastrophes… and this is the major problem that we all face today.As our India is a developing country , but it grows with the fastest rate.Day by Day new inventions occurs. Many machines are made using dif   ferent technologies.some are eco-friendly but some are hazardous to human health . These changes leads to global warming and green house   effect. These all happens because of air pollution which has an adverse effects on climate. India is growing in addition with increasing pollution.combustion of natural gas, petroleum, coal , automobile, aircrafts ,railways, etc produce harmful pollutants like flyash, CO_2, soot, CO, nitrogen oxides, sulphur oxides, CFCs etc.

Due to these pollutants temperature of the earth increases. What we all have to do is to follow some major steps   : 1. Attempt should be made to develop pollution free fuels for automobiles, e.g - battery power , 2. Use of high temperature incinerators for reduction in particulate ash production. 3. Use combustive sources of energy like nuclear power, geothermal power, solar power, tidal power,wind power , etc.

Mona Patel

India's Tough Fight..Growth Vs Climate

Continual Climate Changes, Causing Continuity In Catastrophes…

The Covid-19 pandemic is one of the disasters (virus) which the world is facing right now. We also faced a very horrible cyclone recently called Tauktae. It was the strongest cyclone in the region since 1998 which killed 4000 people. Heavy rainfall, thunde r and wind speeds upwards of 100 kilometres per hour have ravaged several western Indian states due to the cyclone.

It's widely accepted around the world that human activity is affecting Earth's climate. Man has polluted the environment on a large scale. There is no doubt that the planet and atmosphere could one day turn against us.

Therefore we have to take steps forward and stop using plastic materials. It is very harmful, not only for the health of humans but also for biodiversity. By using a recyclabl   e cloth bag, it will help reducing the amount of plastic we use. At the same time we should Save Electricity, Reduce Pollution, Reduce Food Waste and most importantly Stop Cutting down the trees. With a little effort, each of us can do our part in reducing climate change.

Sambardhana Dikshit

Continual climate changes, Causing continuity in catastrophes…
The essence of the beautiful earth is deteriorating
People hoping for sunshine but the fact is that they are succumbing
Fences are becoming short and glaciers are augmenting
The land is now on the verge of disappearing
Still, people's mind and humanity is not surging
It's now high time to understand the   importance of esprit prevailing
Let us change ourselves and others for a peaceful surviving.

Shipra Pandey

Continual climate changes, causing continuity in catastrophes…
We're are chopping down too many trees,
Our earth is in great pain and yelling ' Stop' please please..
We should care, From all our heart, plant trees as much as we can..
Stop using plastic and we can use paper bags as much as we can..
"Use paper bags with care , so our trees don't become rare"
Never burn plastics, save rain water; create awarness..
First step from our side, Then anybody can follow us..
"Have patience "
"People change"
Earth will look prettier and greenery again..

Nafisa Azmin

Climate Change (A Major Issue)

Continual climate changes, causing continuity in catastrophes…

Climate change brings about shift in natural vegetation. Unseasonal rains and rain deficit monsoon have disturbed the crop cycles . India can become a true global superpower in the fight again st climate change , if it speeds up its shift from fossil fuels to renewable energy. Increasing the fleet of electric vehicles and its charging infrastructure in India can be the key to improve air quality in cities . The unstoppable growth of India and it s population these days are causing a harmful effects to the society . So the solutions to be considered are : - changing our main energy source to clean and renewable energy, solar ,wind , geothermal and biomass could be the solution . We must stop defores tation in all forms. It not only worsen the level of carbon dioxide but also the Beauty of the Nature and its habitat.greenhouse gases that are driving present climate change. We can try to minimise the birth rate . India is still battling hard to control over climate changes . As its never too late to save a planet we altogether should take the minimum precautions and control over the usage and make a better living .

Ananya P. Mishra

Continual climate changes , causing continuity in catastrophes …
we are the last generation that has a chance to stop climate change before it is too late. The apocalypse is not something which is coming, the apocalypse has arrived in major portions of the planets and it's only beca use we live within a bubble of incredible privilege and social insulation that we still have the luxury of anticipating the apocalypse. 25 years ago people could be excused for not knowing much or doing much about climate change today we have no excuse sin ce climate change and the global economy now affect us all, we have to develop a sense of the oneness of humanity. What can we do is Say no to plastic, Renewables to the rescue, Whenever possible, use public transport, Switch to electric cars, Reduce food waste, Stop chopping down the forests, Iceberg production affects the mass balance of the parent ice sheets, and melting icebergs influence both ocean structure and global sea level, we can plant trees inside our house, in and around a building. Things tha t we depend upon and value - water, energy, transportation, wildlife, agriculture, ecosystems, and human health are experiencing the effects of a changing climate. What will change us is not technology or science what will change us is the ethical transfor mation of a society.

Payal Kamdi

Continual climate changes, causing continuity in catastrophes…
Continual climate changes, causing a lot of problems in our society and environment too.
The previous precautions are to make the boundaries to collect wat er To plant more amount of trees in drought area As a citizen to take the one step ahead from our home only.
Planting and saving is key step to save our environment.

Abhilash Sharma

एक अनजानी दुविधा :- विकास या ऋतु

Continual Climate Changes ,   Causing Continuity In Catastrophes…
जब करना हो सबका विकास ,
तो डूबती है किसी की आस ,
भुजती है मजदूरों की प्यास ,
ना आती वो कुछ जीवों को रास ,

क्या बढ़ाए विकास की नाव ,
कहीं हो ना जाए ऋतुओं का अभाव ,
पेड़ों के तन पर ना कर जाए कोई घाव ,
हमारे आगे बढ़ने का चाव ।।

Mohanapriya.K

Growth Vs Climate In India

Continual Climate Changes, causing continuity in catastrophes…

Focusing on Climate or focusing on the development of our country? As important as the country's development is, it is also important to regulate the climate and protect the people. People are greatly affected because of climate instability.

Fear of being halved makes people very sad.

People are increasingly suffering from hunger, unemployment and disease. How many deaths occur every day. How can one think about the development of the country alone when all these things are being fixed. Because protecting the people of the country is also the development of our country.

Indu Prakash Deo Pandey

Continual Climate Changes, causing continui ty in catastrophes…

Climate is the long -term average of weather, typically averaged over a period of 30 years. More rigorously, it is the mean and variability of meteorological variables over a time spanning from months to millions of years. Some of the meteorological variables that are commonly measured are temperature, humidity, atmospheric pressure, wind, and precipitation. In a broader sense, climate is the state of the components of the climate system, which includes the ocean and ice on Earth. The cl imate of a location is affected by its latitude, terrain, and altitude, as well as nearby water bodies and their currents.

Climates can be classified according to the average and the typical ranges of different variables, most commonly temperature and pre cipitation. The most commonly used classification scheme was the Köppen climate classification. The Thornthwaite system, in use since 1948, incorporates evapotranspiration along with temperature and precipitation information and is used in studying biologi cal diversity and how climate change affects it. The Bergeron and Spatial Synoptic Classification systems focus on the origin of air masses that define the climate of a region.

Sadiya Siddiqui

Continual climate changes , causing continuity in catastroph es… which has increased the fatality rate since the past decade. In a way or the other, human beings are responsible for these calamities and disasters that the world is facing. Being 2nd top most populated country in the world after China, India is a develo ping country. It is very difficult for a developing country to maintain a balance between growth and the climate. Since the past few decades, we have seen that to catalyze the growth, we have destroyed many jungles and established colonies, multiplex, indu   stries, etc. Industrial waste and other waste are not being managed appropriately. The unmanageability of waste is causing disaster to the water bodies.

Researchers concur that a worldwide temperature alteration is caused basically by human action. In par ticular, the proof shows that specific warmth -catching gases, like carbon dioxide, are warming the world - and that we discharge those gases when we copy petroleum products like coal, oil, and gases. Carbon dioxide is the warmth   -catching gases in our climate answerable for the majority of the warming estimated in the course of recent many years. It's delivered during concrete assembling and when coal, gas, oil are scorched - something people begin doing a lot of during the modern unrest through to the prese nt time.

Princy Carol Gonsalves

Continual climate changes , causing continuity in catastrophes …
Our Environment is a home for many living species
Because of environment we can perform umpteen activities
We will be forever grateful for giving us birth,
Thank you mother earth for providing us with essential resources to sustain life on our planet earth.
Global warming, air pollution, ozone layer de pletion, forest fires, water contamination,
are the consequences of the greedy man.
Instead of planting trees only on the environment day,
one should plant trees every day and take care of them.
All the living species should be valued,
especially the endangered ones need to be protected
We should be grateful for all the resources which we got
free, gifted from our mother nature.
Together we can save our planet, protect our environment
and susta in it for the future.

Jasmine Panda

Bridge Between Life And Death!

Continual climate changes, Causing continuity in catastrophes…
We all are trapped in devastation and destruction,
Global warming, climate change and pollution!
Drought, flood, cyclones and deadly earthquakes!
Engulfed in the monster -like worldwide pandemic!
Submerged deeply in so -called mental instability,
Depression has swallowed everyone of us completely!
Seems like we all are walking in a narrow bridge,
A big question mark between life and death!!!

Simranjeet Kaur

Continual Climate Changes , causing continuity in catastrophes…
it is a bit tough now but soon everything will be right and these problems already begun to impact our planet in more ways than we can think .We just have to control the increasing tyranny and increasing population.Temperatures continue to rise throughout   the planent. The main cause of these catastrophic effects on our planet is pollution.When disasters occur due to these changes, the economic condition of the country is greatly affected.
On the one hand the government has to pay compensation to the victim s and on the other hand the economic system of the country which deteriorates is different. Saving the environment starts with us and it is our responsibility to act against these terrible changes to preserve the planet for future generations. To save the earth from disasters we should take appropriate steps to prevent this problem. We have to save environment decrease deforestation

Flairs and Glairs, a platform by a student for the students. We are esteemed youth struggling to carve out our path for our future and we follow a basic mindset Since everyone is not born with all-round skills. Joining hands with people who are born to execute it with perfection is the best way to evol ve. Self-Evolution is the need of the hour but, evolving as a community is what we strive for. The initiative as kickstarted by, Founder - Mr. Shubham Shah with the motive to utilize the skillset and talent of writing has now a team of 10+ people who are actively participating into newer forms of learning and discovering talents among youngsters. We Provide platform and services like Publishing opportunities, Open mics, Workshops, Hands-on training. Operating with Brand Name of Flairs and Glairs (Publication House), we offer the chance of elevating a passionate writer to an esteemed author   With Brand name Teekhe Zasbaaat. We bring to you an opportunity to get accustomed with the Public Speaking and Presenting of Thoughts along with regular challen ges to brush up your inking spirit.   The newest initiative to extend our services we introduced in a new writing Platform- The Glittering Fables and Ink Over Tears.

We Choose to Fly Like A Falcon than to be

a Leg Pulling Crab.

To Know More: Infoline – 7781900870
Mail Us At-
flairsandglairs@gmail.com / info@flairsandglairs.in
Or Visit is at
www.flairsandglairs.com / www.flairsandglairs.in
Social Handles- @flairsandglairs @teekhezasbaaat